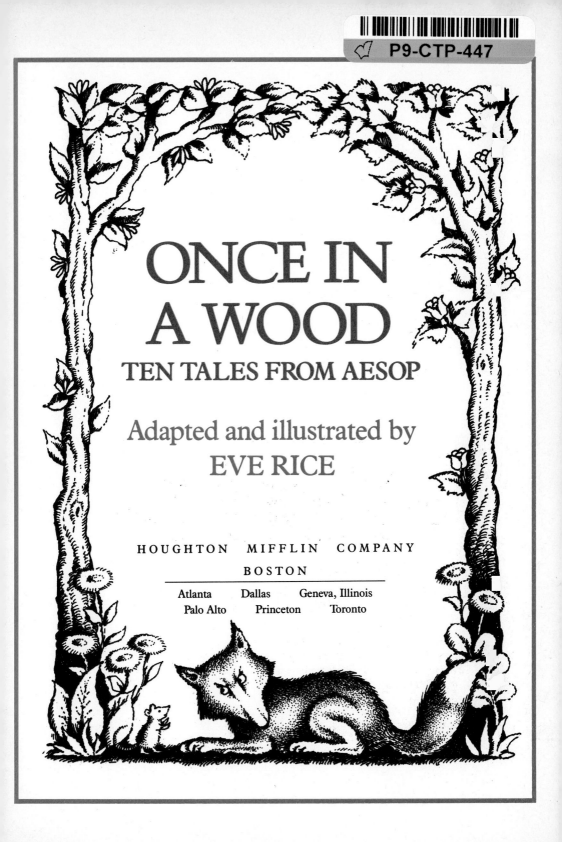

ONCE IN A WOOD
TEN TALES FROM AESOP

Adapted and illustrated by
EVE RICE

HOUGHTON   MIFFLIN   COMPANY
BOSTON

Atlanta   Dallas   Geneva, Illinois
Palo Alto   Princeton   Toronto

This one is for Tim

Once in a Wood: Ten Tales from Aesop adapted and illustrated by Eve Rice. Copyright
©1979 by Eve Rice. Reprinted by arrangement with Greenwillow Books, a division of
William Morrow & Company, Inc., and Curtis Brown Ltd.

Houghton Mifflin Edition, 1993

Printed in the U.S.A.
ISBN: 0-395-61779-0
456789-B-96 95 94

CONTENTS

THE FOX
AND THE CROW

Once in a wood, long ago,

there lived a clever Fox.

One morning as Fox stepped out,

he saw the Crow fly overhead.

In her beak she held a piece

of tasty yellow cheese.

Fox licked his lips.

He had not had breakfast yet.

But Crow soon landed in a tree,

safely out of reach.

"Tree or no," said clever Fox,

"I'll have that cheese, by and by."

Then he said to Crow,

"Good morning, friend.

My! How well you look today!"

Crow flapped her wings with pride.
And Fox declared,
"Why, in my life I've never seen
feathers shine the way yours do.
And such a handsome bird as you
surely has a lovely voice.
Will you sing a song for me?"

So Crow, of course, began to sing.

She raised her beak.

"C-caw, caw-caw."

But as she did,

she dropped the cheese.

It fell right into Fox's jaws.

He ate it up and licked his lips.

And then Fox said to Crow,

"Thank you for my breakfast.

I will pay with some advice:

Beware of those who flatter

and tell lies meant to please—

and be glad, you foolish bird,

you only lost a cheese."

THE LION
AND THE MOUSE

One day, a mighty Lion was
fast asleep in the woods.
Thinking he was just a rock,
a little Mouse ran up his back.
The Lion woke at once
and took the poor Mouse
by the tail.

"How dare you wake me up?"
he roared.
"I am going to eat you!"

"Oh, please," the Mouse said.

"Let me go, and someday

I will repay you."

"Don't be silly!" Lion roared.

"How will you repay me?

You are just a little Mouse—
too small to be
much use to me."
But then he laughed.
"All right. Go on."
He put the Mouse down and
she ran off into the woods.

When many days had passed,
the Mouse ran by that place again.

And hearing an awful roar,

she soon found Lion,

caught in a trap made of rope.

Quickly Mouse ran to the trap.

She took the rope in her teeth

and chewed and chewed until

she chewed right through the rope

and set the Lion free.

"Thank you!" roared Lion.

"You are welcome," said the Mouse.

"And now I hope that you can see

how big a help

small friends can be."

THE FOX
AND THE GOAT

Fox went walking in the woods

and fell into a well.

"This well is very deep,"

Fox thought sadly to himself.

"And I cannot jump very high.

How will I get out again?"

Just then a thirsty Goat

passed by.

"Hello, Fox," said the Goat.

"Why are you down in the well?"

"Oh, Goat," replied clever Fox,
"I came to get a drink, of course.
 This water is
 the finest in the wood."
"It is?" asked Goat.
"It is!" said Fox. "But come
 and taste it for yourself.
 I'm sure you will agree."
So Goat jumped down
into the well.
When Goat had had a drink,
he said, "This water is
 as sweet as it can be.
But tell me, Fox,
 how will we get out again?"

"That is easy," said the Fox.
"If you will stand very still,
　I can climb upon your back.
　And as soon as I am out,
　I will pull you up."
So Goat stood still
and Fox climbed out.

But then Fox turned

and walked away.

"Oh, please!" Goat called to Fox.

"Don't go!

How will I get out again?"

"Don't ask me," the Fox replied.

"You should have looked

before you leaped—

and asked yourself

the question then."

BELLING THE CAT

A hungry cat had come to stay
and all the mice lived in fear.
The mice decided
they would call a meeting.

When they were
all together,
the biggest mouse
stood up and said,

"There is a hungry cat about.
As long as he walks these woods,
not one of us is safe.
So I ask you all to think.
What are we to do?"
Then one mouse gave a plan.
And one mouse gave another.
And still a third had his say
and on and on until
a very young mouse spoke.

"Friends," he said.
"I think that we can
solve this problem easily:

Hang a bell on the cat.

Then we will know when he is near
and we can stay out of his way."

"A good idea!" someone called.
And all the other mice agreed.
"We'll be safe at last!" they said
and danced around until
a very old mouse spoke.

"Friends," he said.

"One moment, please.

Things are easier said than done—
the old and wise will tell you that.
So now, will someone tell me this:
Who is going to bell the cat?"

THE FOX
AND THE STORK

Fox came to Stork and said,

"Will you come to dinner?

I will fix a tasty meal."

"How nice of you to ask,"

said Stork.

"I will be glad to come."

So Stork went to Fox's house.

And Fox cooked the dinner.

He served Stork hot soup

in a plate.

It smelled so good. . . .

But Stork, who had

a long, long bill,

could not eat soup from a plate.

And she watched while

greedy Fox ate up every bit.

"Don't you like my soup?"

Fox laughed.

And Stork went home

as hungry as she had come.

The next day, Stork went
to Fox and said,
"Will you come to dinner?"
"How nice of you to ask,"
said Fox. "Of course,
I will be glad to come."
So Fox went to Stork's house.
And Stork cooked the dinner.

She served Fox hot stew

in a tall jar.

It smelled so good. . . .

But Fox, who had no bill,

could not reach into the jar.

And greedy Fox watched hungrily

as Stork ate up every bit.

"Don't you like the stew?"

asked Stork.

"You set a fine example

when you fixed that meal for me.

I think you should be happy

that I've used your recipe."

THE HARE WHO
HAD MANY FRIENDS

The Hare had many, many friends:
the Crow, the Goat, the Cow....
Everyone was Hare's good friend,
everyone except the Fox.

And every time Hare saw the Fox,
she ran to save her life.

But one day, when Fox came round,
Hare thought,
"Why should I run away?
My many friends will help me out!"
So Hare went to Crow and said,
"Please, Crow. Fox is coming!
Will you hide me in your tree?"

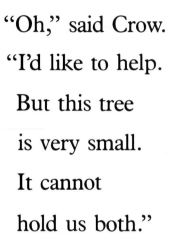

"Oh," said Crow.
"I'd like to help.
But this tree
is very small.
It cannot
hold us both."

So Hare went to Goat and said,

"Please, Goat. Fox is coming!

Will you butt him with your horns?"

"Hmmmm," said Goat.

"I'd like to help.

But I am very busy now.

I have a lot to do."

So Hare went to Cow and said,
"Please, Cow. Fox is coming!
Will you chase him far away?"

"Ah," said Cow. "I'd like to help.
But I cannot chase anyone.
I have hurt my leg, you know."
"Yes, I do know," said Hare.

And then with Fox right behind,

Hare ran to save her life once more.

"Alas!" she said when she was safe.

"Those in trouble soon find out

how many friends they really have.

I once thought I had so many.

But now I see that I was wrong—

for, in fact, I haven't any!"

THE LION
AND THE FOX

The Lion had decided
that he was too old to hunt.
"I cannot run well anymore.
My four old legs are tired.
But, if I use my head,
I'm sure that I can get my dinner."

So Lion went into his cave
and sent out word that
he was sick in bed.
Then one by one, the animals
came to wish the Lion well.
First the Calf came,
then the Horse came,
then the Deer, the Duck, the Pig.

And clever Fox, hearing the news,
also came to pay a call.

"Hello, Fox," Lion said,
  looking out his door.
"Won't you come in
  and stay awhile?
  We can sit and talk a bit."
"Thank you, sir," Fox replied.
"But I will not come inside."
"Afraid?" asked the Lion.
"You should not be—
  for I am old and sick,
  as you can see.
  Please, Fox. Do come in."

"What I can see," Fox replied,
"are footprints by your door.
  They show that many went inside—
  and none came out again.
  So thank you, Lion, just the same.

Though fools may
walk into danger
when the signs are all about,
this Fox will not come in until
your other guests come out."

THE CROW AND THE WATER JUG

One day thirsty Crow
came upon a water jug.
"Now I will have a drink,"
she thought.
She put her beak into the jug,
but the water was so low,
Crow could not get a drink.

So she reached farther in.
She flapped her wings
and stretched her neck.
But still she could not get
a single drop to drink.

"I know," she thought. "I'll turn
the jug over on its side."
And then she pushed
with all her might.
But no matter how she tried,
the jug still stood upright.
"I may as well give up," she thought.
And crow might have flown away—
but she stopped and thought again.

A moment later, Crow bent down

and picked up a pebble.

She dropped it in the jug

and then she bent

and picked another. . . .

One by one, on and on,

she dropped the pebbles in the jug.

And with each stone
that she dropped in,
the water rose a little bit
until, at last, it reached the top.
"Caw, caw!" Crow called
and had her drink.
"Caw, caw!" Crow called
and flapped her wings.
For she had learned
that many things
are better done bit by bit.
And things that can't
be done by strength,
may often be done by wit.

THE FROG
AND THE OX

A young Frog came hopping home
as fast as he could go.
"Father!" he told the old Frog
sitting by the pond.
"I have seen the biggest beast—
a beast as big as big can be!"

The young Frog pointed
toward the meadow.
"Look, Father. There he is!"
"Nonsense!" said the old Frog.
"That is just the Ox.

And he is not so big at all.

Why, with a breath of air or two,

I could be about his size.

Watch me. I will show you."

With that, the old Frog took a breath

and puffed up his chest.

"Am I as big as the Ox?"

"No, Father," said the son.

"I'm sure the Ox is bigger still."

So the old Frog breathed again

and puffed himself up some more.

"Am I as big as the Ox?"

"Oh, no," replied the son. "Not yet.

The Ox is bigger still."

At that, the old Frog took a breath
and puffed himself up even more.
"Am I as big as the Ox?"
"No, Father," said the son.
"I fear the Ox is bigger still."
"Nonsense!" cried the old Frog.
"I must be bigger than the Ox!"

And then, like the fool he was
(fools try to be what they are not),
he breathed in all the air he could.
He took more air
than he had room.
"I must, I must,
I must, I . . . Oh!"
And then
the old Frog burst:
KER-BOOM!

THE COCK, THE DOG, AND THE FOX

The Cock and the Dog

set off through the woods together.

When darkness came, they found

a tree where they could stop

and spend the night.

Cock climbed up to the top

while Dog made a bed below.

And so they slept till dawn
when Cock awoke and crowed,
"Cock-a-doodle-do!
Cock-a-doodle-do!"
Now clever Fox,
who was nearby,
thought,
"Aha!
It is the Cock.
What a meal
he will make!
I'll just use
a trick or two
to get
him down
from that tree."

So Fox went round and called,

"Who was that?

Who sang so well to greet the day?

I'm sure I'd like to greet the singer."

"It was I," replied the Cock.

"Cock-a-doodle-do!"

"Who?" asked Fox. "It is too dark.
Come down so I may see you."
"Oh, I'll come down," Cock replied.
"But you must ask the doorkeeper
if he will open up the door.

You'll find him
underneath the tree."
"Of course," said Fox and
smacked his lips.
"I will ask him right away."

So Fox walked around the tree ...

but he only found the Dog.

And Dog bit him on the leg.

"Oooch! Please, don't!

Oh, stop!" cried Fox

as he ran off into the woods.

Cock laughed to see him go.

"Good-bye, you silly Fox!" he called.

"You know at least a hundred tricks,

but now you've learned

something new:

Even the Fox can be outfoxed!

Cock-a-doodle-doodle-do!"